WELCOME TO MY NIGHTMARES

SALVATORE J. LO MONACO

ISBN: 978-0-578-30717-6 (Paperback)

Any references to historical events, real people, or real places are used fictitiously. Names, characters, and places are products of the author's imagination, and any resemblances to actual events or places or persons, living or dead, is entirely coincidental.

Front cover image by Jessica Hennings.

Illustrations by Jessica Hennings, Susanne Crow, &
Bella Lo Monaco.

Edited by Susanne Crow.

Printed by IngramSpark, in the United States of America.

First printing edition October 2021.

For Devon and Bella.

Hold on tight to your dreams.

And never let go.

CONTENTS

WHEN SHE CALLED   1

THE GALLOWS   6

MEDINA   16

LONELINESS   21

MORTIMER   23

BROKEN   26

SAMUEL   27

THE LONG ROAD HOME   30

IT'S JUST NATURE   32

LIGHTHOUSE   44

THE BOY WHO LOST HIS SMILE   45

SHE FALLS   52

BIG BROWN EYES, GOODBYE   53

A DELICACY TO DIE FOR   55

A NEW BEGINNING   62

NOT IN THIS LIFE   63

NIGHTMARES   77

A MONSTER ATE MY HOMEWORK   78

ACKNOWLEDGMENTS

To be honest with all of you, I never thought that any of my works would be worthy of publication. It took quite a bit of mettle and encouragement to follow my dreams and put myself out there. So here we are, at the pinnacle of bringing my deep (and sometimes dark) imagination to life.

I'd like to thank my family and friends for putting up with my melancholy while I searched for my writer's identity and voice. Just like the flowers need the rain, sometimes the writer needs the pain. Thanks for understanding and supporting me.

A special thanks to my editor, Susanne, for sifting through pages of devious twists and turns, pointing out better ways to spin my webs to entice my readers. I could not have done this without your guidance.

Of course, I need to thank my exceptional illustrators, Jessica, Susanne, and my own daughter Bella (who insisted that I *only* use her shortened name in my book). Thank you so much for your hard work in capturing the tones of my stories and poems. You are all so very talented, and much appreciated.

Lastly, I thank you, my 'haunts', for your eagerness to read and want more from me. I hope you find what you are looking for within these pages. For some say, these are what dreams are made of…

WHEN SHE CALLED

Jake mainly lived on his brother's sofa; an old, tattered leather Chesterfield dating back to the mid-19th century. The upholstery had worn thin, just as much as Jake's mental health throughout the years. Jake spent most of his young life defending his country, only to return home battered, bruised, and broken, to a world who seemed to no longer want him around.

His wife and boy deserted him while he traversed foreign soil, pushing back against the insolent few that remained as his marked enemies. His home was sold from underneath him, foreclosed in a deal still under wraps by bureaucracy and buyouts. And so, Jake laid there on his brother's couch, popping 800 mg ibuprofen like breath mints, watching the world go by in ever slow motion.

One particularly uneventful Saturday, Jake awoke to the sound of a distant voice coming from his cell phone, clutched in his gnarled right hand. With bleary eyes, he glanced at the time stamp on the call: 2:47 am. The voice on the other end sounded familiar and persistent, albeit drunk.

"H…hello?" Jake muttered over the stammering voice on the line. He starting to rouse, and a small panic rushed into his adrenal glands. "Lynn?"

"Babe?" The female voice questioned, anxiety stirring in her own voice as well. "Honey? Babe? Are you there?
I love you! Babe? Why won't you say it back?

Honey?"

Before Jake could say another word, the line went dead.

"Lynn? LYNN???"

But there was no answer.

Jake attempted to call the number back but could not find it on his contacts page. Stupid phone, he thought. He dialed the last number he remembered he had for Lynn, but the number he dialed was no longer in service. Just as much. How long had it been? Fifteen? Sixteen years? Why was she calling him now, after all this time?

Sleep never returned to Jake that evening. He rose from the sofa, pacing, wondering, worrying. What if she was in some sort of trouble? And now she needed him. Wanted him. Wanted him? After sixteen years? Last time he saw Lynn, she was shacked up with a flighty squadron jock, someone she wasn't in love with but couldn't say no to. But now?

Sunlight dawned through the sheer white veneers, translucently lighting up the living room where Jake dwelled. Jake was already roused, looking through old photos in a shoebox he kept for no reason at all. There she was, in all her glory; the Lynn he remembered from way back when. Such a pretty-young-thing, pouty lips, and big, beautiful brown eyes. Those eyes always held him at bay. He never knew if they were beckoning him to come hither or warning him to stay away. Such mysteries he never did find answers to.

Searching through the shoebox found no solace, as Jake was unable to locate any address or forwarding phone number for her. He'd already woke his brother, asking stupid questions he already knew his brother couldn't answer. All he had was the distant memories, faded photographs, and that call.

Sleep evaded him for the next couple of nights. Jake waited up with hopeless abandon, wishing he would hear from Lynn again. But she never called. He sat there on the antique sofa, countless games of solitaire won and lost, draining his cell phone's battery to the brink each time, hoping, praying, wishing for that phone to ring. Nothing but the awkward silence of his own pining heart.

"What is wrong with me?" Jake wondered aloud, not for the first time in his life. "Why this obsession with this chick? I'm going insane, that's it." Jake thumbed through his phone and found the number for his therapist. "Tomorrow, I will make an appointment, and set my mind straight. And hopefully get something to help me get some sleep!"

Morning came as always, and Jake rubbed his tiresome, sleepless eyes. He called and made an appointment with his therapist for that afternoon, then set out to maintain some sort of hygienic ritual.

"Had I really been neglecting myself over all of this?" Jake wondered, as he washed a week's worth of funk from his body in his closet-sized shower. He even took a razor to his face and shaved for what seemed a decade, patching the nicks with pieces of toilet paper here and there. After consuming a meager breakfast of granola and yogurt, Jake set out for his appointment downtown; he decided a nice walk in the fresh air would help ease his troubled mind, rather than listening to saddening songs and even sadder news on the radio of his beater.

Jake finally arrived at his therapist's office around eleven forty-five; his appointment was scheduled for noon. Despite the crisp air and the gentle strides, he took, he just couldn't seem to shake that overwhelming feeling of Lynn. He sat down with his therapist and spilled it all: the past, the present, the call. The fact that he cannot sleep. His therapist, being a psychiatrist as well, prescribed him a dose of sanity, and something to help him catch some z's. She listened to him, gave some advice on his subconscious, warning him to not get too attached to his past. Jake took everything in stride, only half listening while anticipating a good night's sleep for once. By the time the exchange was completed, Jake was out the door, and on his way back to his sofa.

As night fell and the stars began to twinkle, Jake prayed one final time for that moment to repeat itself. Just once. Just so he could tell her how he felt. He held his phone in his hand, gripping it while the pain gripped at his heart. With a shot of whiskey, Jake swallowed his sedative, and sleep grasped him like an old, estranged lover.

The time was 2:47 am.

"Honey? Babe..."

That voice!

Jake woke with a start, his hand still gripping his phone, his thumb still pressed to the screen as…

"…Are you there? I love you! Babe? Why won't you say it back? Honey?"

With bleary eyes he looked down at his phone, before the line went dead.

VOICEMAIL

Then he remembered.

It was 16 years ago that Lynn perished in an automobile accident. She decided to drive herself in a drunken state, because she could not reach anyone to take her home. Even at 2:47 am.

Jake never did forgive himself.

THE GALLOWS

Sometimes, a shadow crosses a man's heart, and at that moment, he knows he is going to die.

Joe and the old man sat across from each other in a dusty cell, in a dusty town, somewhere on a dusty, forgotten map. Joe looked up from his hands, large and calloused, and stared into the eyes of his neighbor. The old man, greying in all the right places, stared back at him.

"How are you feeling, Joe?" inquired the old man. He flossed out his greying beard with withered hands as he waited for a reply.

"Same as usual." Joe responded. His brown hair bristled in the dank air of the cell, and he blew it back into his normal side-part. His deep brown eyes never left the gaze of the old man's slate grey ones.

"I reckon", said the old man. "Seems daybreak is upon us." The old man stood from the cot he was set upon and stretched his lower back. The sound that echoed off the cinderblock walls reminded Joe of a goat chewing on an old, rusty tin pail. "Guess we should be on with it."

Joe rose from his side as well, his burly build tapping into his already arthritic knees. Although Joe was only in his mid-forties, he felt older somehow; not wiser, but experienced.

"I suppose we must." Joe blandly stated.

The jailer moved nimbly, keeping his bold blue eyes upon both men as his keys jangled against the cell door. Both Joe and the old man egressed from the cell and walked the half mile stretch towards the doors leading to certain freedom. A small gust of wind drafted the foyer, and both men were greeted with the wafting smells of something cooking. Something delicious, the old man digressed, and soon the two men shuffled their way out in the direction of the smells.

A despairing display of geese crossed their path, honking and pecking the barren ground. A sole rooster welcomed the light of the sun with his brash crowing. And speaking of crows, a single, black-feathered bird perched himself upon the belfry top of the small church in the center of town. Its beady eyes stared down at the interlopers. The two gentlemen, hankering for a morning meal, made their way towards the café.

The morning sun cast webs of dust particle beams across the dingy café, resting upon the abundant bosom of the caretaker of the establishment. Emma, a portly woman of no credible discernment, stood at her bar, wiping half-moons without much thought. The door creaked loudly as the gentlemen entered.

"Help you?" Emma murmured, still unconsciously wiping the counter. The wonderful aroma of baking bread and greasy meat sidled from the vast kitchen area beyond her post.

"Breakfast", stated Joe, "and some strong coffee to wash it down with." Joe and the old man sat at the bar, Joe's cumbersome weight causing the ripped stool cushion to let out a pronounced 'woof'. The old man hesitated, then spoke up.

"Eggs will be fine, Em. Scrambled. Also, some of your fine Applewood bacon."

"And you, Joe?" Emma asked without really caring. "Whatcha eating?"

"Same for me, I think", Joe answered. "Two sugars and cream in that coffee, Em."

Emma spat and polished a mug from the filthy cupboard, then poured a dark, viscous liquid from the pot attached to the stationary percolator. She dropped two crumbly cubes of sugar into the mug, then set it down in an almost grimy saucer before Joe. Emma brought out some half-and-half containers that seemed to be missing their coldness from refrigeration. Joe thanked her with a nod.

"Something to wet your whistle?" she asked the old man. He shrugged and offered to have what Joe was attempting to swallow. Emma just sighed and poured another mug of the sludge. The old man declined any lightener or sweetener; he preferred his cup as dark as the crow's feathers. As Emma disappeared into the kitchen, the old man turned to Joe to begin his query.

"So, Joe", the old man started, "tell me your story again. From the beginning." Joe appeared nonplussed to retell such tragedy, especially an additional time to the old man. Nonetheless, Joe began as he always did, from the start of what he could remember.

"Do you recall back when, as the market crashed, and it seemed economic life was going to regress back to the dark ages?" Joe asked, rhetorically. "Well, my story circles around that time. My life was stable: married, two kids, house with a white picket fence. But stable seldom means simple. Especially back then."

Joe stopped for a moment, regarded his coffee, and thought better of swallowing more of the same. The old man listened with intent ears.

"My twin boys were just about eight years old", Joe continued. "They were always getting into some sort of trouble. My wife, bless her soul, kept a great home for us all, despite the constant strife. You see, I served honorably in the Army; however, trying to acclimate back to civilian life was a struggle for me."

Emma emerged from the kitchen with two heaping plates of scrambled eggs – a bit runnier than Joe liked – and nearly burnt bacon slices.

"Toast?" Emma asked wanly. Both gentlemen declined. Joe forked his eggs hungrily into his salivating mouth, disregarding the charred meat on the plate beside them. The old man munched on his bacon, moving his eggs from side to side on his plate. Joe wiped his mouth with some recycled (and sort-of used) napkins and continued his story.

"The wife and I fought sometimes. Nothing downright physical, but the emotions and mentality was always negative. She always tried to keep our arguments away from the children. I, on the other hand, have no filter, and let loose as the day was long." He shoveled another mouthful of eggs into his waiting maw, chasing it down with the cooling coffee. "Sometimes the fights were about the kids; their grades, their manners, their disobedience concerning their father. When times were tough, I started drinking. Heavily. My wife hated that part of my lifestyle, you know."

The old man looked up from his meal and just nodded. He had heard this story before.

"It always seemed to keep the demons at bay", Joe stated. He looked down at his unfinished plate with minor disgust, then looked over at the old man's. The old man ate vigorously, brushing pieces of bacon from his grey whiskers. "It was the drinking that ruined my marriage. That drove her away."

Joe sat there and thought a bit, wrenching his hands together to pop a few of his knuckles. Just an old habit that he was unable to break. The old man nodded, prodding Joe to continue.

"At one point, the DUI's piled up, and my driving privileges were suspended." Emma slapped the bill upon the counter and walked away from the conversation, unamused and indifferent. The old man reached for his wallet; however, Joe was quicker to the punch. "I got this one, pal", he said.

"Always a gentleman", the old man countered. Both Joe and the old man sipped a final taste of their coffee and walked out of the café.

The crow flew from the top spire down to the well outside of the café, letting out a long, dismal caw. It watched the two gentlemen casually stroll the main street, walking towards the old barber shop. An antiquated, disheveled striped pole sat idly in front of the shop. An older, more disheveled man greeted the two as they approached his establishment.

"Come in! Come in!" said the rotund, balding barber. His thick black beard matched his even thicker accent. "Greek, perhaps", thought the old man to himself. The barber wiped his brow, sweat glistening from his shiny head. Joe and the old man entered the shop; the barber smiled his practically toothless grin.

"Who first?" he asked, clearing off the station. The old man shook his head and took a seat in the lobby area.

"Just me, then", Joe stated, and slid his burly body into the barber chair. "Gonna be a day, Hector. How about a little off the top?"

Hector smiled again, getting to work with his electric shears and scissors. Half an hour passed, and

Joe looked like a new man. This time, the old man beat Joe to the punch, and had payment ready for the barber. Hector, however, declined payment.

"For you boys today, is free", Hector smiled his toothless grin at the gentlemen. The old man frowned at this, sliding his money clip back into his breast pocket. With a wave of appreciation, Joe and the old man left the barber shop. The crow perched itself upon the non-working barber pole and let out another ghastly caw.

The old man ushered Joe towards the tailor's, and both gentlemen eased their way inside. Joe started up his last conversation with the old man, right where he left off. The tailor, a large man standing over seven feet tall, began measuring Joe's arms, legs, waist, and hemline as Joe spit out his soliloquy.

"The bitch of it all", Joe stammered, tears stuck in his thoughtful eyes, "was picking up the two boys from soccer practice. The boys looked well enough: well fed, well mannered, and well disciplined. But the lack of a father figure at their home really messed with their mental state."

The tailor continued his work unabashed, pulling textiles from here and there, fitting Joe for a jacket with matching slacks. He did so without comment, yet with a precise mind.

Joe choked back some tears, and his voice faltered on his next verse.

"It has been five years since I picked them up that day. Five years since I had a single drop of alcohol. Five years since I drove those innocent boys while drinking. I miss them immensely."

That fateful evening, five years prior, Joe wound up in a drunken car wreck that killed two innocent boys – his boys – and left the oncoming driver paralyzed. Joe never forgave himself. The old man nodded yet again; he had heard this part of the story before.

The tailor finished his business, wished the gentlemen a good day, and informed Joe that he would see him again "real soon".

In the dusty town square, on a dusty mid-morning, in a little dusty town mostly forgotten on some dusty map, Joe and the old man approached the hangman's gallows. Joe was first to speak, save that of the curious crow and its heckling caw.
"Looks like we have arrived", Joe said solemnly.

"Suppose so", replied the old man.

"Caw!" repeated the crow.

A rusty tin pail stood before the long stretch of rope; a small reminder of days long gone. The old man stepped upon the pail and raised himself full upright, looking Joe fully in the face for the first time. Joe stood there, looking back at the old man, anticipating what comes next.

The wind shuddered, and the crow fell silent, watching the two men stare at each other. The hangman's noose shook in the wind before being placed around the guilty party's neck.

"I suppose it is time", Joe said.

"Suppose you're right", said the old man.

The crow remained silent.

"Last words?' asked the old man. Joe silently nodded.

"I reckon I'm sorry for killing my wife", the old man whispered as Joe slightly kicked the pail from under the old man's legs. With an audible 'SNAP', the old man's neck contorted before it broke, dangling him from the gallows pole like a spider blowing in the wind. The crow flew on the same wind, taking the old man's final message to whichever entity would listen.

Joe stood there, perplexed in his own thoughts.

"You know", he stated to no one in particular, "I never did learn his name."

WELCOME TO MY NIGHTMARES

MEDINA

It was particularly cold for an early March morning. The sun peaked shyly from the clouds, draping a single dust beam across the length of the bedroom. Medina was already awake, wide eyed with a perfect smile that discounted the rest of her alabaster skin. It was a special day for Medina; a day she knew all too well. Her smile did not grow any wider, even though her birthday was upon her. She had other concerns to fret about. She was awaiting Mother.

Mother was always interfering in her life. She always wanted to know all about Medina's misgivings. Where was Medina going so late at night? Why was Medina failing her subjects? What was that musky smell in her underwear drawer? Who was that boy with the charming brown eyes and fast motorcycle that always seemed to call at a quarter to nine each evening? When did Medina start fancying dark mascara and brighter-red lipstick? What happened to her little girl who used to wear pigtails, and cute chiffon dresses without worrying about boys, and always minded her Mother? These were the kinds of interrogations Medina loathed, and just knew that this day would be no different. No, this day would be far worse than all the rest.

The bedroom doorknob jiggled, then went silent. A bronze key was inserted into the lock and wrenched the tumblers while turning clockwise. Outside, it started to lightly rain. Medina continued her smile, preparing for the onslaught, as Mother opened the door, and entered the room.

Mother was a lanky woman, as tall as she seemed so prematurely aged. What were once golden locks now dripped with greying circlets, tucked into makeshift curlers on top of her creased brow. Mother's choice of garb this day was simple: an olive dress with patchwork near some of the faded seams. Slowly and with great, painful effort, Mother crossed the threshold, and turned on the light switch to her right.

"Don't you ever knock, Mother?" Medina said cynically, her smile still dancing on her face. Mother did not respond; she just approached Medina's desk and began to straighten the multitude of novelties and dust-covered trinkets that threatened to spill about the ashen-colored laminate below. Medina stared in wide-eyed amusement.

"So, we are going to give me the silent treatment?" Medina declared. "On my birthday, no less? The one day I expect you to lay the compliments and judgments as thickest as thieves, yet you choose to ignore me?"

Mother turned in her direction, slightly, reached down to fetch a bauble once purchased by Medina when she was thirteen (it was a faded cherry lip gloss, now molded after years of use and misuse, and frank abandonment) and pitched it in the overflowing trashcan besides the desk. The rain fell harder now, enveloping any sunlight that once entered the bedroom earlier. Medina would not be discouraged; she knew she had her Mother where she wanted her. The rain just amplified her mood.

"All these years, Mother, you cared enough to tell me how I should feel" Medina began, still beaming that perfect, red-lipped smile. "You lectured me on who I could be with, who I could date. The tone of make-up my skin was permitted to wear. The length of my skirt. If I should go out. When I should come home."

Mother moved on to the dresser now, clearing her path from the desk and upturned hamper filled with ripped blue jeans and dank, half sleeved hair band t-shirts. Atop the dresser were several picture frames, several in shattered fractals due to frequent mishandling. A specific picture of Medina and Mother lay in tatters, neatly piled to the back-left corner of the white oak dresser. Mother carefully gathered the pieces together and placed them in the trash can along with the rest of the rubbish, ignoring Medina's declamation.

The rain fell even harden. Mother moved to the window and closed the drapes, sealing off the outside world. Medina's auburn hair splayed gracefully across her shoulders, and she smiled broadly at her Mother.

"You know, Mother, I'm an adult now." she said. "I'm eighteen. I no longer have to do as you say. I no longer have to listen to your rules. I am free to do as I wish, even if you do not approve. I can date who I want. I can wear as dark of make-up that the boys like me to. I can go out late and come home later. And there is nothing that you, or anyone else can do about it. Nothing."

Mother turned from the window, and looked directly at Medina, seeing her for the first time this morning. Medina smiled, knowing that she would finally acquire her Mother's attention.

"I deserve respect, Mother." Medina stated. "I demand it. Say something!"

Tears formed in Mother's eyes, and her brow creased even further. Mother reached for the light switch and dampened the only source of brightness in the room. The raindrops pattered passionately against the siding, pawing at Mother's heart like a harpist does to his strings.

"Happy Birthday, Medina" Mother croaked with a tearful voice. "I love you immensely and miss you even more. How I wish you were still with me." With a sob, Mother turned the bedroom doorknob, opened the door, and vanished from the darkness.

Medina continued to smile, as only a portrait on the wall could.

SALVATORE J. LO MONACO

LONELINESS

And here I lay again all alone

    Nothing new, always on my own

Voiceless pain in a constant drone

    I call your name but you're not at home

Won't leave a message on your phone

    I'd rather listen to the dial tone

You were here, but now you're gone

    A distant memory fades like the dawn

And now I wish just not to mourn

    A loss I feel from a heart that's torn

Wonder if you'll hear the words I've sworn

    Screaming silently through lips forlorn

Why does it seem the dream will never end?

    It leaves me hanging here by a thread

Terrors subdue into my sightless mind

    Lusting for hope becomes eternally unkind

Time passes slowly but I still count the years

    Still laying here, drowning in my salty tears

MORTIMER

Mortimer sat there in his overstuffed red recliner, his crude mass oozing over the sides of the filthy upholstery. His parrot, Fred, danced eagerly on one talon, nestling his beak into unclean feathers. The antiquated CRT Television sat at an angle, spewing nothing but static and snow. Within the realm of drunken schemes and mimosa dreams, the room reeked of nothing but putrid debris and decay.

A loud pounding sound came from nowhere and everywhere all at once; it startled Fred, who fell from his perch onto his own bird dropping splattered bottom of his iron-wrought cage. Half of the cage stood on its own end, as Mortimer tried to twist it back into shape with a rusty pair of needle nose pliers to no avail. The pliers scampered off the table with each pounding, skittering onto the soiled linoleum below.

"Fer Gawd's sake, door's open!" Mortimer hollered from his chair. Fred continued to get antsy, hoping from foot to foot.

"Mort is death. Death is Mort." Fred repeated this over and over as if summoned to do so on the whim of being offered a cracker.

"Shat up, ya stupid boid!" Mortimer screamed at his pet. "If I could see ya, I'd strike ya down!"

The pounding continued, faint, yet louder still. Fred spread his grimy wings and flapped them aimlessly.

"Mort is death. Death is Mort". Fred continued to chant.

"Whut dids I tell ya, filthy boid?" Mortimer bellowed from his chair. "Door's open!" he repeated to the interlopers making all the ruckus. "See yer own ways in."

With finality, the front door came crashing in. Men in white coats rushed, then sidled back when they glimpsed the scene.

The EMT's were called for a wellness check on Mortimer, who was not seen or heard from in weeks. When they arrived in his home, the EMT's found Mortimer dead of a heart attack, sitting *almost* pristine in his leather chair.

Fred was halfway in and out of his cage; his right talon caught on its edge, nearly ripped off and dangling like that of a one-legged duck. Fred spoke nothing more – he was too busy devouring one of Mortimer's eyeballs, cracking the milky whiteness between his beak.

BROKEN

Life isn't what it used to be
Living a lie serendipitously
Waiting for that moment of sheer honesty
Dreading the night no one could foresee

Been hoping for a new take on things
Looking through such dirty window screens
Unable to see the good for whatever that means
Longing only thoughtless within our dreams

Cynical mind left to think alone
Carving your initials in this heart of stone
Wondering if you still care while you're not at home
Desperate desire through such a capricious tone

Listening to the words that will never be spoken
Love and affection merely a forgettable token
Wringing out a heart filled with tears that have soaked
in
Marveling if I will always be this broken.

SAMUEL

Another cold and bleak Sunday morning graced this seemingly endless month of March. Samuel just lay there, head resting upon his small satin pillow. His chestnut brown hair was neatly combed to the left; parted as his mother always insisted since he was six years old. He was fully dressed to the nines - Gucci black and white pinstriped suit with the wingtip shoes he purchased while visiting Rome during his high school graduation getaway last year. Another Sunday. Another day of repentance. And was he repentant? Why, sure, he should be. After all, it isn't every day you wreck your father's favorite Trans Am after a spell of heavy drinking at the Spring Frat Party. Thunder rolled in the distance as Samuel continued to lay there.

His eyes remained closed; his lips pursed as if in thought of his actions from the 'mixer'. Truly, Samuel was anticipating what would come next; he had yet to face his parents about his drunken adventure with the car.

"And what of it?" he thought. "I'm a man now, right? Eighteen years old, and fully functional!" Hell, men and women his age were getting killed overseas for defending a country he loved so much. He bet service men and women were even allowed to consume alcohol over there, and at an earlier age as well. So why was this such a big deal? His father had great insurance! Only the best for his family. Surely, the vehicle would be covered. Besides, it was only a car.

Samuel didn't recall being wounded at all in the

wreck. If he had, the numerous beverages he imbibed must have softened the blows. Nothing a little makeup couldn't cover before it was time for church. Light rain began to patter on the roof as the door slowly opened into the room. Samuel continued to lay there, silently dreading the moment that his interrogations will begin.

The soft melody of organ playing filled the room as the door opened, reminding Samuel of his mother's favorite Gospel ensembles. His mother must be gearing up for today's 'holier-than-thou' sermons, and how they must be directed at her derelict son. He could smell her sickly-sweet perfume as she approached. He kept silent and still, waiting for his mother to bash him upside the head, or reproach him with scripture. Neither happened, which surprised him. His mother simply kissed his cool forehead while rustling his hair a bit.

"I am being silently rebuked" he supposed. He could not bring himself to open his eyes and face his mother. The rain picked up its pace, no longer keeping time with the organ's melodic tone.

With long strides and heavy footfalls, Samuel's father entered the room. Samuel could sense the change in atmosphere to that of an intense, almost fearful magnitude. His father always drank, always scotch, always in a glass, seldom with ice. Samuel hardly knew his father; he credited his mother for helping him with his studies, his sporting accolades, his 'girl troubles' and 'love interests'. His father's presence was equated to discipline. A hard hand, and even harder love to bear. Samuel hated him, yet respected him all the same. And now here he was, to exact punishment for destroying what little was left of Samuel's dignity.

Samuel's father loomed, stroking his dark, wiry mustache. Again, Samuel fought the urge to face his father, and just lay there with eyes abandoned from the light, forestalling his sentence. And again, Samuel was met with forbearance; his father's paces echoed off the tile back the way they came. The organ music ceased abruptly on the heels of another rumbling course of thunder. Samuel aptly listened to the silence around him and picked up on a voice he remembered from his childhood. Was that really Father O'Malley? Samuel didn't dare to open his eyes to scoff at this notion.

"What would that Irish priest be doing here, now?" he asked himself. "Is this some kind of intervention? I mean, yeah, I'm a little young to be drinking, and I know I shouldn't have been behind the wheel of the car afterwards, but this? This is a bit absurd!" Gradually gaining confidence, Samuel decided to finally face his congregation. Through lips that felt parched and sewn together, Samuel demanded to know what the hell was going on here.

Father O'Malley finished his eulogy, and secured Samuel's casket shut, forever.

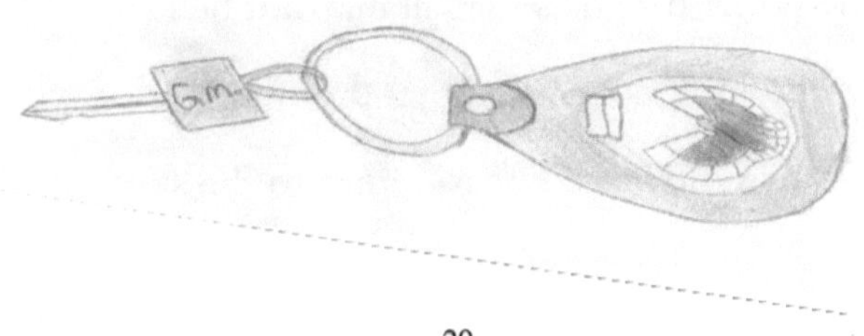

THE LONG ROAD HOME

Watching that stretch of horizon

    The sun setting lower each passing gaze

And I wonder just how far I've gone

    The world has changed these fleeting days

Yet my heart still aches for you

    Like the calling of the sea that I roam

Always longing for tomorrow

    Taking the long road home

Remembering love's sweet soft embrace

    A gentle caress without signs of strife

As days gone by missing your tender touch

    Craving for one last breath of life

My mistress, she beckons, always takes me away

    Keeps me desolate, forever lonesome

Though honor prevents me from running adrift

    I yearn for that long road home

The horizon signals that all may not be lost

    So look not out on that drooping sun

For my time has come to return to the start

And boldly finish what I yet have begun

Through wrinkled hands and mind uncured

Working feverishly as time grows old

Setting sights for that distant shoreline

Finally taking that long road home

And when my time comes, as it shall

Please bury me not beneath the cold blue foam

Send me home in a flag draped pinewood box

Send me down the long road home

IT'S JUST NATURE

Allen Jones always hated family outings. Especially when these outings involved more natural settings, sans electronics. Pushing his larger-than-normal lensed glasses back upon the bridge of his nose, Allen saddled his blue, one-strap pack upon his back and stepped outside his front door. With a few nimble swipes, his cell phone came to life, and began loading his latest saved game.

"Oh, no you don't", exclaimed his mother, a broad woman with an even broader expression on her face. She greedily snatched the cell phone with large fingers on her left hand, wagging her right index finger at Allen in distaste. "This is going to be an electronics-free outing, Al. We discussed this at supper last night."

"But Mo-om!" Allen whined, trying hard not to sound younger than 11 years old. "I was just about to beat my all-time record in Candy Crash!"

The lift gate of their baby blue station wagon slammed shut. Allen's father looked up from his chore of loading the family vehicle, and wiped the sweat from his receding, dusty blond hairline.

"Son, mind your mother", he stated, not delicately. Intertwining his gnarled fingers, Mr. Jones cracked his knuckles in such a loud fashion, almost to say, 'That's the end of the discussion.'

Mrs. Jones continued her abashment, stuffing the cell phone in her oversized linen tote.

"Al, you need to get out more. You are missing out on life, being stuck indoors with all these…electro-whosiewhatsits! Why, when I was your age, we didn't have all this gadgetry and hoot-a-nanny. We went outside, enjoyed the fresh air! My stars, it's just nature, Al! It won't kill you!"

Allen subconsciously started scratching the nape of his neck, as he often did when his mother bore down on him about his excessive introversion. At least he was entertained, his mind was occupied, and his eye-hand coordination was not found lacking. But his parents, children of Generation X, would never understand this concept, let alone his impending boredom during the however-long car ride he was about to endure.

"But Mom!" Allen insisted, "What about the long car ride? What am I supposed to do then?"

Mrs. Jones scoffed at her son's ignorance as she ushered Allen towards the rear passenger side of the vehicle.

"Why, Al! Look around you! Just look at all the scenery! We aren't driving that far…your father can make it to the beach in roughly two hours. Why don't you gander at everything you've been missing by being cooped up indoors. Gaze out your side of the window. Don't be afraid, Al! It's just nature!"

Mr. Jones settled in the front driver's seat and set the GPS for Patterson beach, a mere 2 hours, and 25 minutes from the Jones' driveway. Mrs. Jones climbed in the front passenger seat, her ample girth causing the family vehicle to groan in protest. Allen slammed his door shut, folding his arms about his scrawny chest in his best 11-year-old angst.

"Seatbelts", his father reminded everyone. Mrs. Jones struggled with hers, naturally. Allen buckled quickly, then returned to his arm-crossing stance. Mr. Jones slipped the wagon into reverse, backed out of the short driveway, turned onto the main street, and headed in the direction the purple arrow on the GPS directed him.

As suburbia subsided into a more likeable countryside, Allen unfolded his arms and invoked his powerful imagination to help pass the time. At first, he was immersed inside his favorite match-three game with the cutesy candies, watching chocolate spattered fish and exploding gummies clear line after line in his mind. Thoughts like these always made him happy; sickly sweet, unrealistic, yet satisfying accomplishments. His escape from reality.

"Look over there, Al!" his mother boomed out of nowhere, begrudgingly pulling him back to the here and now. "Remember when we used to hike on the paths near those woods? We should do that again soon…"

Allen remembered it all too well. Swampy marsh was more like it, surrounded by what should be trees if they ever grew leaves. His mother 'insisted' that he should go on a walk with her to help her exercise, to get out more. "It's just nature", she would say. Only, this nature walk placed Allen in the hospital for three whole days. Who knew that not only was Allen deathly afraid of those winged, sardonic, yellow-black striped demons of the sky, but he was also deathly allergic to their venomous sting? As the itch on the back of his neck intensified, Allen scratched without abandon.

The drive coursed forward towards Patterson beach. Mr. Jones was in the zone, making greater time than the GPS expected. Mrs. Jones opened her enormous tote and removed a curvy bottle of coconut scented sunblock. Splatters of white and greasy goo chortled from the bottle onto her bulky arms and upper chest, spread by sausage-like fingers to her face and dabbed on her button nose. The entire car reeked of fresh piña colada, soured only by fear-sweat caused by Allen's not too distant memories.

The hospital stay wasn't all that terrifying for Allen. Once the many doctors were able to start him breathing again, Allen had received his first cell phone as a gift from his mother. Perhaps it was an accolade of guilt on her part; after all, it was her idea to drag him along on that outing. The phone was meant to be a gesture of safety, in case anything would ever go wrong, Allen would have the means to call someone. That is, if his nose wasn't buried in some flashy app, wasting her son's precious time and energy. But Allen, like many children his age, loved these types of gadgets. Reveled in them. A reminder to forget; to escape.

"Look there, son", his father beamed, breaking Allen's morose thoughts. As the purple arrow on the GPS became more prominent, the Jones' wagon crept up on some familiar familial haunts. "The sign says we're getting closer to the beachfront. Remember when we came out near here for the company picnic?" Mr. Jones seemed very bemused thinking about his work and time spent parading his family like trophies. "What a great time we had. We really should have placed second…"

Allen did remember that awful picnic that year. The year his father almost defeated his boss at the father-son competition. What Allen lacked in strength, he seemed to make up for with cunning, plotting, planning; his ability to not only think outside of the box, but to act quickly before an opponent realized there wasn't really a box present. Allen thought he owed this newfound alertness to his technological obsession. Of course, his mother disagreed. His neck throbbed a bit, but Allen dared not scratch for now.

One of the final obstacles at the picnic was the rock-wall climb. Mr. Jones, a tried-and-true athletic junkie in his younger years, was ready to put his boss to shame, and complete the course in record time. His team was only down by two points, and winning this round would declare his team, and his family the winner by a point. Only, who knew that Allen was deathly afraid of heights, to the point that even standing on a three-foot ladder would cause him to shake? Allen did try his best, despite his mother's agonizing belittlement ("He's too small and puny to pull himself up the wall!"). But in the end, Mr. Jones would have to rescue his fear-frozen son from the rock-wall, halfway to the bell, and the glory and honor beyond. The Jones family never finished the competition, never placed in the finals, and Allen never lived it down from his mother.

"If you would get out more", she would taunt him, "you would be able to climb anything! Trees, hills, mountains…the shed! You could even help your father put up the Christmas lights! You should be enjoying life, outside, like a normal boy. It won't kill you! It's just nature."

With a flick of a wrist, Mr. Jones applied the wagon's right directional signal, indicating an almost imminent arrival to their destination. The purple arrow was replaced by a slowly growing checkered flag, and the GPS lady started barking orders to turn this way and that. Allen was amazed that time galloped as fast as it did. Mrs. Jones forcefully rolled down her passenger-side window, excessively damaging the already tattered plastic handle. Salt-spray wafted through the opening, mingling nicely with the coconut lotion.

After a few turns and slowdowns, the Jones' family wagon finally came to a halt in a parking spot close to the boat ramps. Allen read the quaint sign above the lot: **'WELCOME TO PATTERSON BEACH'**. There weren't too many other cars in the lot this afternoon, even though the weather was clear, and it promised to be another fine day for beachgoers. None of it mattered to Allen though. He just wanted to placate his parents, then get back to busting candy wrappers and lollipop traps.

Mr. Jones was first to exit the vehicle, stretching his

long legs and popping the small of his back. Mrs. Jones followed; the wagon either moaned in ecstasy or sighed with relief of her departure. Disgruntled, Allen was last to disembark, not looking forward to the sandy walk of shame, nor what lies beyond. All three Joneses carried their belongings and made their way towards the dunes.

Blue sky and bluer waters greeted them as the Joneses made their way towards the beach. Mrs. Jones set up the lounge chairs and blankets, with a red and white polka dot parasol borrowed from the neighbor for some shade. Mr. Jones plopped the cooler down on a corner of one of the blankets, reached inside and drew himself out an Orange Crush. Allen sat down on a blanket, dead center, and marveled at the great blue yonder in front of him. Yes, he could hear children laughing, music playing, and the deep call of the waves beckoning him to succumb to a watery grave. His neck playfully itched, nagging at him like an elderly mistress.

Allen saw himself submerged in the water, waist deep, unable to see his lanky legs beneath him. Without warning, a school of jellyfish scuttled by, their nettles brushing against his bare skin. He screamed, oh he screamed, but his voice doesn't carry; the breath taken from him very much like the aftermath of the bee sting. But the pain…the pain seemed so unbearable…and he couldn't breathe.

A beach ball smacked Allen straight in the forehead, bringing him back to here and now. His father looked on at him with a lively smile. "Come on, son. Let's go toss the ball around a bit. Bet it would be cool out there in the water. Whattya say?" Allen continued to sit there, unamused, wiping sand from his hair and brow.

"No, thanks. I'll just watch for now."

Mrs. Jones paid no attention to her boys. She laid there in her lounge chair, allowing the sun to gently kiss the parts of her skin that wasn't coated in her body butter. Dejected, Mr. Jones sulked off to the water's edge, and dove through an incoming wave.

Allen watched his father dive into the incoming wave. What he saw after that was troublesome. Not just to an 11-year-old, but to anyone watching someone in the water. When Mr. Jones reemerged, a large great white shark closed in on him; a toothy, double-rowed grin opened and primed to swallow him whole. Allen tried to scream.

"Al, hon. Can you bring mommy a diet soda?" Mrs. Jones asked her son behind large red sunglasses. Allen looked back at the water, expecting to see bloody horrors and what could be left of his father. Only, his father was laughing, tossing that stupid beach ball with another child in the water. No shark. No blood. Well, of course not. Sharks couldn't get that close to the shoreline. Could they? Allen shook his head, stood for a moment on wobbly legs, and fetched his mother a diet cola.

The day was getting later, and Allen's fear of the unknown lurking in that deep blue was growing heavy on his conscious. The 'what-ifs' and 'could-bes' were getting the best of him. He wanted to experience what he was missing. He wanted to show his mother that he wasn't such a coward; that he could be a 'normal' boy and do 'normal' things.

As Mrs. Jones snoozed in her chair, Allen marched towards the water, waited for the next sufficient wave, and dove headfirst. Allen almost immediately opened his eyes, half expecting the salt water to burn. Strangely, his sight was unhindered, as he breathlessly admired such an underwater view. He swam for what seemed like hours, gaping at the many colors and shapes. All kinds of fish and vegetation, corals and sea life, lined row after row like in his favorite game. He loved the openness of being down here, wishing he didn't have to return to the surface for air.

Allen, knowing his lung capacity was not as strong as most 11-year-olds, started to ascend to the surface. Only, the faster he swam, the slower he sank to the bottom. Looking down, Allen found it harder and harder to visualize a bottom to this underwater world. His lips started to chill first, then his toes. In the distance, a light glimmered, and drew closer. Two icy cold skeletal hands grabbed at him, pulling him under further.

"Ok son, time to pack it in." Mr. Jones was gathering their belongings in a neat, sandy pile. Mrs. Jones looked at Allen with such pity, then at her husband in an 'I told you so' demeanor. Allen continued to process what he saw yet didn't see. The water was still there, with its non-menacing, welcoming embrace. And here he was, unscathed, embarrassed, and a tad bit curious.

"Mom?" Allen whispered. "May I please go out into the water? Just for a minute? I promise I won't bother you about the phone on the ride back. I just need to…see something."

Astonished, Mrs. Jones shook her head yes. Mr. Jones stood and watched his son remove his t-shirt, socks and sneakers, and gingerly walk towards the water line. Adrenaline coursed through his veins as Allen approached the wetter sand. He knew he had to do this; to prove to his mother, to prove to himself that he wasn't a coward. After all, it's just nature.

Allen dipped his toes into the water and was met with a slight chill. To Allen, it was fascinating. He stepped even further into the water, when large hands grabbed him and pulled him back towards the shore.

"Al, honey, we almost forgot to put on your sunscreen", his mother stated with unending overprotectiveness. The familiar curvy bottle was already in her hand, plopping the white lotion into her meaty palm. She slathered the sunblock about his scrawny chest, arms, legs, and his face like she had done a million times before. Allen felt like a greasy mess. Mrs. Jones allowed him back into the water after only 10 minutes, disregarding the 15 to 30 minutes someone should wait after liberally applying the lotion.

Allen returned to his stance at the waterline, then stepped in further, feeling that electric chill run up his spine. He allowed himself to be immersed even further, this time to his waist. The water trickled across his arms as he swam out a bit into the waves. Allen plunged his head into the water and abruptly jumped back up, laughing as the bitterness teased his taste buds. His eyes burned slightly, but he didn't care. Allen found something that he enjoyed. Something that didn't harm him. Something that didn't emulate from an electronic device. No, that something was just nature.

The Joneses started heading back to the family vehicle, excited yet exhausted from a day at the beach. Allen, especially, was overtaken by his newfound courage. For once in his life, Allen was able to face his fears. And that was an accomplishment far greater than matching candies.

The itch at the nape of his neck became unbearable. On the way home, Allen nonchalantly picked at the blackened scabs, causing the open sores to ooze and bleed. By the time they reached home, the cancer that was unbeknownst and left untreated, had spread to his already feeble lungs.

To everyone else, Stage IV Melanoma was such a tragedy for this family.

But to Allen, it was just nature.

SALVATORE J. LO MONACO

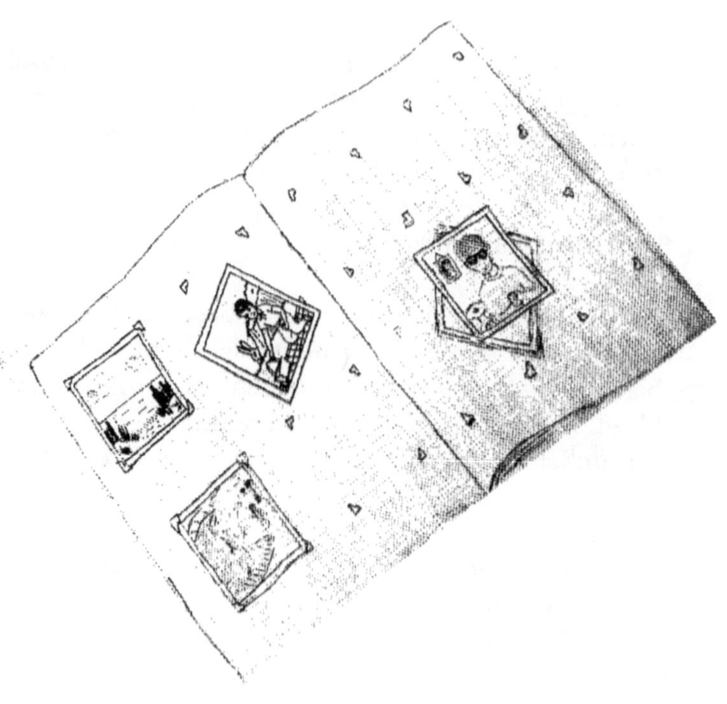

Lighthouse

She holds a manner about her
That sight goes unseen
    A brightness
    A shine
Some sort of gleam
Without her guidance
That shelter from the storm
Vessels lost at sea
Another sailor less warned

Always quick with a smile
And heart-borne tenderness
    A light
    So precious
Some star nonetheless
In turn goes 'round
As dawn fades to eve
Rip currents a-gather
Yet fear left reprieved

Endlessly grateful
Her light outstretched for all
    With it hope
    Within it desire
For those who answer her call
Without her guidance
That shelter from the storm
Vessels lost at sea
Another sailor less warned

The Boy Who Lost His Smile

There once was a boy who forgot where he last saw his smile. Each day as he woke, he searched for where he may have misplaced it. The boy searched his pillowcase; he found nothing but broken dreams and garish nightmares. He searched under his sheets; however, he found nothing but a growing boy who was afraid to become a man. He didn't dare search under his bed or the confines of his closet; nothing but monsters and skeletons awaited him there. No, the boy remained disheartened; he had really lost his smile.

One non-particular morning, the boy woke from yet another dream – a bad one, at that – and tirelessly rubbed the sleep out of his eyes until his corneas were a tad bit sore. Swinging his legs over the side of his racecar bed, he slid his stockingless feet into his panda-faced slippers with ease. Thankfully, no monsters attacked him from under his bed.

The boy's pajama top, riddled with spaceships and planetary notions, was damp with fear sweat. He never liked fear sweat; the distinct odor from such always made him feel too young and too vulnerable. Unbuttoning his top took some effort, but the boy disrobed and tossed the stank-tinged shirt into a waiting hamper.

He stood there for a moment, half naked, half deciding whether to don his favorite t-shirt displaying his favorite Pokémon, or to finish removing his near soiled, matching bottoms. Choosing the latter, he kicked off his slippers before stripping down to his skivvies.   Modesty withheld; the boy dropped his drawers with the slightest shake of his bottom. He reached for his dresser, opened the top drawer, and procured a neatly folded pair of tighty whiteys. "Nope", he thought, "my smile isn't in the dresser either."

The boy pulled the t-shirt over his head and flailed his arms until they made purchase with the armholes. He then went to his closet (no skeletons, he hoped), opened the French doors slowly, peeked inside (no skeletons this time) and snatched a pair of blue jeans from a rusty metal hanger. Pulling the pants on one leg at a time, the boy dressed himself all prim and proper. He slid his feet back into his slippers, turned towards his bedroom door and exited his room, making his way downstairs to the tiny kitchen. Delightful aromas of salty bacon and eggs cooking wafted up the stairway.

His mother stood at the little stove, carefully frying uneven slices of bacon while scrambling a few eggs in a separate pan. The smell alone made the boy salivate, and his stomach growled as he sat at the small kitchen table. One of his panda slippers fell off his foot and hit the cold linoleum floor with a noticeable 'PLOP'. Startled, his mother turned to see her boy, and smiled. The boy was envious; where *did* his smile go?

"Momma", he started, "have you seen my smile?"

His mom bristled at the question, and her smile grew longer across her face.

"But of course, my dear. It's always there, on your face." She shifted the eggs in the pan until the yolks hardened further. Just as he liked them.

"I can't find it, Momma", he stated defiantly. "I know where it used to be, but it isn't there now."

The boy's mother frowned at this. She knew the boy was having a tough time with everything lately but didn't expect him to act *this* way.

"Well," she commented, "Where do you remember seeing it last? Perhaps if you trace your steps, you'll be able to find it again."

This sounded like a great idea to the boy. His mother scooped up eggs and laid bacon slices on a waiting glass plate and placed the meal in front of her son. "Eat up, baby", she said. "You're going to be late for school."

The boy scarfed down his eggs while toying with the salty slices of meat on his plate. School. His second least favorite life event. He was certain that he was going to have to take a Science test; Science being his first least favorite subject. Finishing breakfast, the boy rushed back to his room, slid on some socks (forgetting he was one panda slipper shy) and his Nike sneakers, then grabbed his one strap book bag. He stopped at the bathroom door and convinced himself to at least brush his teeth and comb his hair.

Trotting cautiously down the stairs, the boy reached the landing, gave his mother a quick kiss on the cheek, and headed out the front door just in time for the school bus to pick him up at his driveway. He carefully stepped up and entered the hungry maw of the bus, enveloping him in sounds and odors of pubescence.

All the seats on the bus were either taken by other boys and girls or being saved for incomers from additional stops. The back of the bus, a place so dark and desolate, appeared to be mostly vacant, save that of a few thugs and bullies the boy knew all too well. With a sigh, the boy made his way towards the back, hoping he would not be noticed.

"Where's *my* lunch money, twerp?" One of the bullies exclaimed at the boy. He just recalled that he forgot the lunch his mother had prepared for him in the fridge and was now a bit concerned how this incident would turn out. Having no money to hand over, the boy shrugged, and waited for the onslaught from his least favorite bully.

"No money?" said the bully. "Well, I suppose I will have to take it out of your hide later."

The boy cringed as the bully reprimanded him. Not only would he be hungry later, but probably nursing a black eye, or even worse, a trip to the toilet – headfirst. The bully laughed and prodded his acquaintances to do likewise. The boy realized that his smile was never there on the bus.

Upon arriving at school, the boy rubbed at his newly wet-willied ear and disembarked. Hurriedly, he ascended the twelve steps before him, and entered his least favorite institution. Hundreds upon thousands of kids blocked the way to classes and bathrooms; or so it appeared to the boy. Pushing his way through the masses, the boy found his classroom and slowly entered. Yep, it was Science first thing. And he was correct in his assumptions - there was a test today. No smile could be found in that classroom; that was for sure.

Time ticked by slowly, and before he knew it, lunch period was upon him. As the boy entered the engulfed hallway, he was accosted by his not-so favorite bully.

"Fork it over, small fry." The bully held out his grimy hand in expectation of receiving a bagged lunch. The boy looked down at his sneakers, embarrassed, ashamed, and alone. The bully caught on to this and readied himself to make a big scene.

"Aw, mommy forgot to pack your lunch, didn't she?" The bully ridiculed the boy. But the boy just stood there and took it, knowing what hell would await him if he were to retaliate. None of this mattered to the bully, who reached out and grabbed the boy by his thin arms.

"That's ok, shrimp", the bully snapped, "I know just how to quench your hunger...and thirst!"

With that, the boy was forcibly escorted to the bathroom marked 'Gentlemen', and was dunked headfirst in the nearest, open stall. "Nope", recounted the boy, "no smile in here either."

The rest of the day dragged on; the boy tried desperately to hide the bathroom odor wafting from his wet head. His classmates kept a large distance from him, murmuring how disgusting he was, how weak, intimidated, and scared. The boy just prayed for the day to end so he could return home to his mother and give up on his search for his smile. He was determined that the smile was gone forever, like his matching socks when placed in the laundry.

The bell finally rang, and the boy walked the stretch to the school's exit, hoping to get a seat on the bus far enough away from the bullies. Of course, his small stature was pushed out of the way, and when he embarked the bus, no seats but the back aisle were available. Slinking down further than he thought he could, the boy endured the mockery and humiliation from the back.

The bus crept its way along its route, dropping kids off at their driveways. The bully gave the boy one last noogie before reminding him to double the lunch money tomorrow. Finally, the boy arrived at his stop, alighted the bus, and slowly walked up the driveway to his house.

His mother was waiting for him at the stoop, a large grin on her pretty face.

"Welcome home", she said. "I have a surprise for you, waiting inside."

Bewildered, the boy entered his house, and was met with one of the biggest amazements of his life.

There, sitting at the kitchen table, was a clean-shaven man in his Dress Blues; a military man with his sea bag standing upright at his high-gloss polished shoes.

"Daddy?" the boy whispered, then ran to bury his face in the man's chest. Ribbons and medals – accolades from a war being won – hung from the man's uniform. The boy cared less to notice.

"Hello, son. I have missed you so much!" his father said through tears streaming down his face.

The boy looked up at his father, and smiled, a great big smile that reached from ear to ear. And that is when he realized he never lost his smile, after all.

SHE FALLS

Traipsing cold feet, to even colder floor below.
Slipperless, her footing slips, and her gait is no more.

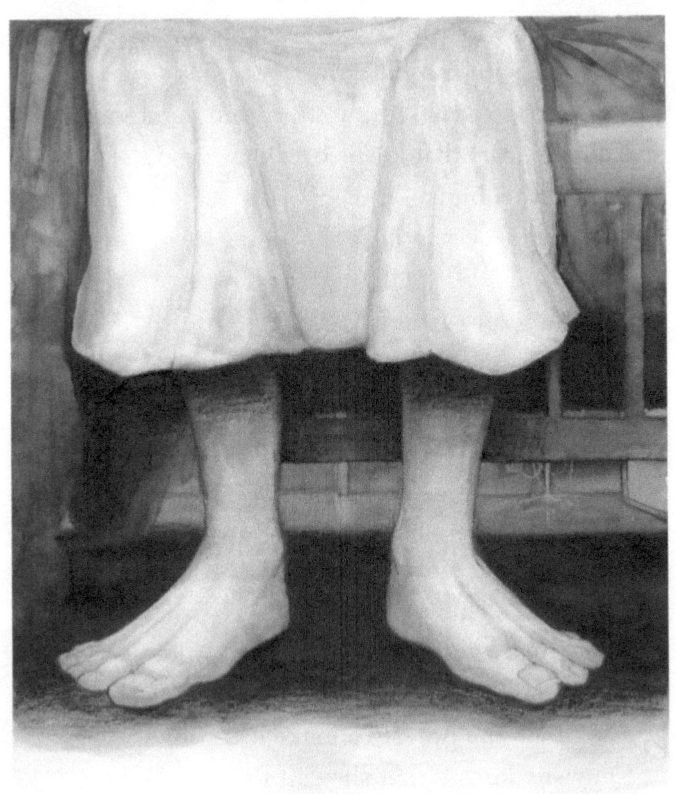

BIG BROWN EYES, GOODBYE

As the morning dawns and you start to wake
Along with the sun's most early rise
Dreams that come have gone before
Just like the shadows left behind
Watching those long-lost summer days
Seem to vanish right before your eyes
Teardrops form without a soothing embrace
Telltale heart that keeps breaking inside
And with a blink –
Big brown eyes, goodbye

Reaching out again with fingers spread
Stretch to the heavens far and wide
Longing for something, lusting for more
A gentle feeling powerless to hide
And still she searches, her eyes on the prize
Silently screaming through candied lips forlorn
Another web weaved through her despise
And with a shudder –
Big brown eyes, goodbye

She holds the power to make it through
Only she knows that she can fly
Yet courage comes on the edge of a wing
And she knows that she must try
Never lose hope, never give in
For forever is within her sights
And just remember –

Big brown eyes, (never say) goodbye.

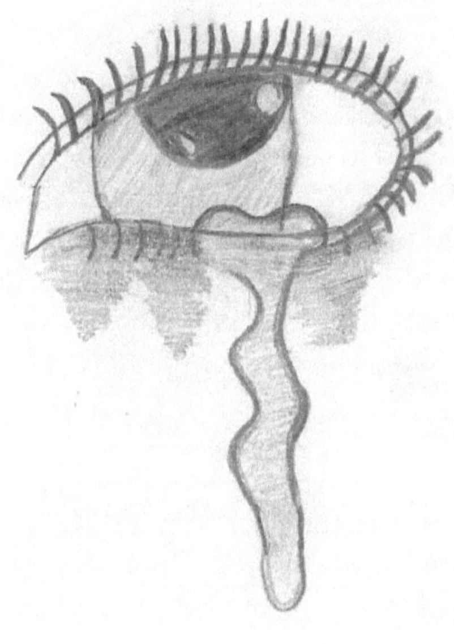

A DELICACY TO DIE FOR

(For Dr. Jasiczek; may you find these 'Milloy-isms' as entertaining as ever.)

Millicent enjoyed all things exquisite: from her glamorous movie star style of hair, down to the lacey stilettoes that adorned her perfectly pedicured feet. Born and raised in a gated community, far off in a New England suburb, Millie was sheltered from most things 'simple' and predominantly pedestrian. Some say she was born with a silver spoon in hand, gilded with fine textiles inherited from a long line of royalty. Others just knew she exalted royalty; Millie was a self-made queen.

Having made her fortune from a glorious and successful run at the cosmetic industry, Millie found herself wanton to travel. Not just her lust for international byways; Paris left her loveless and hateful for the evenings, Milan left her high and dry, and she would never discuss her time spend on the sands in Rio. A northerner like her wanted more and more to stay state-side and try her luck with more of a southern flair. Hopping in her baby blue Cadillac, Millie pointed herself towards the coast, aiming for something she just hadn't experienced yet.

Taking I-95, Millie traversed the New Jersey Turnpike with selfless abandon, feeling freedom for the first time in her life. She imagined she was a race car driver, battling for the pole against many others in humbler vehicles than hers. And the trucks! So many of them on the open road; she chose to ride with and sometimes against them, just for sport, until the wee hours of the morning came. Pushing into Delaware, Millie found a rest stop and lightly snoozed for a few hours; however, the adrenaline still pumped through her veins like wildfire through the Amazon.

Millie finally found herself in Northern Virginia, with signs for the great spans of the Chesapeake Bay Bridge Tunnel beckoning her further. Bridges never frightened her, even as a child with stories of trolls who lived under them. But this one tickled her fancy a bit; both in a good and in a bad way. There was something about that bridge she was unsure about. Determined, she pressed on.

Crossing into Virginia Beach, Millie decided to stop and take in the sights, right off the bridge's descent. A small, run-down restaurant stood there, seemingly boarded up in case of a hurricane. The parking lot was deserted, save that for Millie's baby blue Caddie. A modest sign hung on the door.

'OPEN', it proclaimed.

Millie turned off her vehicle, debarked, and cautiously stepped inside the restaurant. Inside, she was met with the most beautiful, most tasteful, most intricate anything her senses could ever form into words.

For a run-down restaurant on the outside, the establishment held a five-star appearance within its bosom. A large crystal fish tank embellished the great hall, filled with the most exotic sea life known to the

Eastern shore. All brass work was polished to a gleam; stainless steel and glass a plenty shone in every booth as well. The place was empty but had the feel that it could fill up at any moment. Millie strode further in, past the hostess podium, and further into the fray.

"Can I help you?" A male voice rang out from the kitchen area. Millie thought she made no noise but realized her heels must have knocked acoustically on the planked floorboards as she walked.

"Um, I was just…curious." She responded, a little more timid than she wanted to be.

"Curious…" The male voice drew closer, then a figure appeared from behind the kitchen door. A balding man wearing a dirty white apron graced Millie with an aloof smile. "Hi, I'm George. I own this greasy spoon."

"Millicent." Mille thought of extending her manicured hand, but thought better of it, seeing the slimy mess crawling up George's arm. "Millie, for short."

"Pleased to meet you, Millie." George grabbed a few towels from behind the waitress supply station and began wiping his mess onto them with the grace of a Sherman Tank. "So, what brings you to Ol' Virginny?"

Millie blushed at the rhyme, thinking it cutesy yet gooberish. Seeing she was close enough to the extravagant bar setup, Millie pulled up a bar stool and set herself down, almost exhausted.

"I'm vacationing." She explained. "Tired of the North, actually. Just wanted to head out on the highway and see the sights."

George chortled at that.

"And you picked Virginia Beach?" George went behind the bar and started to fix Millie something that resembled a Cosmopolitan. Millie watched with astonishment as he did so, not missing a beat as he shook and stirred. He offered an olive, which she neatly declined.

"I choose where and when I stop, thank you very much." She replied, not so kindly. George didn't notice and handed her the drink.

George and Millie spent most of that afternoon bantering about the North versus the South, collegiate teams, driving principals, and who could arm-wrestle the other more elegantly. George told Millie of his days spent as a peanut farmer in Suffolk, long before his culinary calling. Millie shied from her cosmetology business and relied on her beauty and brains to carry her through conversation. For George, it was like a dream come true; a female never came to visit his establishment and just shoot the shit with its proprietor. For Millie, however, she felt like she found a kindred spirit she could call her own. As night began to brood its purple gaze through the windows, Millie realized she was not only hungry, she was famished.

"Hey Georgie?" She slyly instigated, knowing she'd

strike a chord with her new friend. "Care to dine this fine wine of a girl with something she's never had before?"

"Now you're talking, Yankee Rose." George retorted, slipping himself back into his familiar domain. "Ever had Shrimp and Grits before?"
Millie wrinkled her nose. "Grits? As in corn meal?"

George's laugh was full and quite charming. Millie fell in love in an instant. "Why yes, Millie, but the way I prepare my most infamous meal, you would never know it was such a beggar's banquet."

"No, Georgie, I have never had Shrimp and Grits. Delight me". Millie was intrigued, and ravenous.

George smiled, and got to work, sautéing giant prawns in his best peanut oil, infused with decadent spices. The grits he cooked special with Australian butter and twice strained goat's milk. The delicate, tempting, delicious smells from the kitchen began wafting through the restaurant. Millie's mouth watered.

Soon, George emerged from the kitchen with two heaping bowls full of Shrimp and Grits. He placed one in front of Millie and smiled.

"Bon appetite, compliments of the Chef." He said with a wink.
Millie ate frivolously, hungrily, scooping spoonful after spoonful into her waiting mouth.

"This…is…DELICIOUS!" She exclaimed through mouthfuls, chewing on perfectly cooked prawns, tasting the creaminess of the corn in every bite.

George watched her eat as a loving companion, goading himself to boast and brag.

A reddish rash appeared near Millie's upper lip and started to spread.

"Oh, Georgie! You can cook for me ANYTIME!" Millie moaned, gleeful at her almost finished meal. She was even thinking about seconds, when her throat began to close, and she started choking on a rather large prawn.

"Millie? Are you ok?" George got up from his seat to try to help. Millie started to convulse, her face blemishing a deeper reddish-purple as the air trapped itself inside her lungs. Large pustules started forming on her face and neck and began to splurt into her bowl.

"MILLIE!" George started slamming her on the back, thinking she was choking. He attempted the Heimlich, but to no avail. After calling 9-1-1, George tried CPR with a facial barrier from the First Aid kit he kept in case of these emergencies. By the time the ambulance arrived, Millicent had died.

George attended the funeral in that sweet suburban town, far away in New England. Although he only knew her for just a day, he felt he owed that much to her. He sat there, in his best suit, next to a woman who looked just as classy as Millie herself. It was her sister, Joy.

"I'm so sorry for your loss." George began, introducing himself to Joy. "I wish I would have known she was allergic to shellfish. I never knew."

"She wasn't." Joy scoffed, dabbing her eyes with a small lacy hankie she kept in her breast pocket.

"She was allergic to peanuts."

A NEW BEGINNING

As the rain cascades softly
Pattering the windowpanes mostly
Washing away the pains within you
Finding another day to continue
Restless soul

Harken, there's a new dawn without envy
Wiping the tears away, and trembling
Not knowing what this day shall bring
Ears plugged from voiceless sounds that sting
Hopeful grace

Special beyond anyone's repertoire
More bountiful alone than for any man's desire
Rising above, know your worth is grand
So much that the rest don't dare to understand
Take your place

Never forget just where your road has taken you
Look not back, but to the light that shines before you
A new beginning, the wind calls out once more
And only you, dear heart, know how to even the
score
Moving onward

As the rain cascades softly

NOT IN THIS LIFE

(For Ron; thank you for taking the time to sit and tell me your stories every day. May you always be forever young.)

Ron entered the Silver Dollar Diner one simple Sunday autumn morning, his most desired spot to set down and eat since his latter teenage years. Now at 86 years old, he longed for that nostalgia, as well as a slice of apple crumb pie, and his all-time favorite: a large root beer float, with a shiny maraschino cherry gracing the top of the perfectly rounded whipped topping. Not some glop you could squeegee of an aerosol can, mind you; that whipped cream had to be hand-made, and boy, did it ever taste like it was! Saddling up to the counter, Ron sat down at his usual corner spot, ordered his usual fare, and rested while waiting for his treat. Thinking he was alone at the bar; it took but a moment for Ron to realize that someone else was fancying his every move from across the way.

"Good morning, Ronald." The mysterious female, dressed in a gorgeous black lacy gown, gave Ron a nod and a wink. Ron looked around, scratched at his near-white hair underneath his blue U.S. Air Force cap, and blushed.

"Hey! I…uh…I, don't think I know you." Ron stammered a bit, bewildered that this woman knew who he was. And why was she approaching him, in his favorite place, near his usual spot?

"I've seen you around here, Ronald," she started, noticing his bafflement among his curiosity. "I figured I would come over and introduce myself. You know, get to know you a little better."

Ron was having a hard time looking at her. Not that she was grotesque; this woman was quite breathtaking. No, Ron thought, that wasn't it at all. Her entire being just kept…changing. One minute it seemed like she was five feet two inches tall. The next, she towered the room at almost six foot. Was she wearing a floppy black hat when she sat there a minute ago? Where did that hat go suddenly? And now…now it's back on her head! The dress, is it lace? Leather? No, it's lace. And her eyes. Can someone's eyes really be purple? Or are they blue? Ron's head started hurting.

"Don't fret, dear Ronald." The woman got closer to him still, and he could see a little clearer. Yes, she had on a floppy black hat, the type women often wear in the springtime during Easter, if it would have been white. The dress matched perfectly, and yes; it was definitely lace. But her eyes went from purple to blue, then back again. That he was certain about.

"What is your name, Miss?" Ronald backed away a bit, and almost fell off his stool. The waitress brought out his pie and float and paid no further attention to what was going on at the bar. The pie looked delicious enough, but Ron lost his appetite. The root beer was cold and crystalline in the frosty mug, as dollops of the whipped cream began falling off the top onto the counter. The woman stole the cherry from the top of the float with a fell swoop of her black fingernails, chewing carefully on the fruit, stem and all.

"My name is Catrina", she replied, taking a seat right next to Ron. She could sense his discomfort, and a smile played at her lips. "Why don't you eat your pie, Ronald? We have much business to attend to."

"Business?" Ron was puzzled. It was Sunday. As far as he knew, all he had to do was go back home and walk his dog, maybe play Scrabble with his daughters. "What business?"

"Oh Ronald." Catrina stirred Ron's float with his straw until the ice cream began to melt a little. "The littlest things we forget in our old age. Tell me, what do you remember most about this place?"

Ron sat and thought for a moment, not wanting his pie or his float anymore. He used to take his wife of 60 plus years to this same diner. That was, until she died almost a year ago. He sure did miss her. Not just her in a sense of physically being with her, but her companionship, her laughter, her scent. This woman, Catrina, was really pulling the old heartstrings right now, and he did not appreciate that.

There were other memories that started coming back in droves about the diner. Some were distant, like the fog on the mountains. Others were right in front of his face. But what exactly was Catrina looking for him to share? She seemed to be there at the diner for a specific reason. And Ron needed to craftily figure it out before he wasted any more of his time.

"Well," Ron began, "what do you want to know? I have been coming here for as long as I can remember and have quite a number of stories to tell." Ron saw the gleam in her (purple? blue?) eyes and thought he had her where he wanted her.

"Well, Ronald, I do love stories." Catrina crossed her long, black panty-hosed legs (she was around five foot eight) and seasoned herself for some storytelling. "I think we have time to listen to a few."

Slowly and steadily, Ron began telling his tale.

"I remember a time when this old diner housed all of us football players from the high school." Ron sat up straight as he spoke, removing his cap as if the tale was a solemn oath. "Me an' the boys had just won a hard match against the 'Cootesville Cougars'. Boy, I remember the day as if it were yesterday…"

The Greenstand Gladiators were down by 5 points late in the 4th Quarter, when Ron took the snap from his husky center. The pigskin flew into his hands with a THUD, and Ron scanned the muddied field, looking for an open target. Only 25 yards to the opposing end zone, with hardly a hope of winning the game. And there it was, by the grace of God, a path left by a beam of light shining from a hole in the clouds…beckoning Ron to run right through it. And so that's what Ron did; he ran, straight on through, dodging tackles, spinning through gloved hands, and jumping over bruisers with the poise of a ballerina Neanderthal. He dove headfirst into the muck, and as time expired, scored six points after crossing the goal line.

The Gladiators celebrated that evening with root beer floats and greasy burgers. Ron was celebrated as the MVP, and Quarterback of the Year. All the locals tried to fill the diner to capacity that night, just to get a glimpse of the Quarterback hero. Ron sat in the corner stool at the bar, guffawing along with the rest of his teammates.

"You know," Ron said, remembering that great time in his life, "that was the first time I ever had a root beer float." Ron looked over at his melted concoction on the counter and wrinkled his nose. "I still love those things to this day."

Catrina stared wildly at Ron while he finished his story. Not because the story was all that interesting. Ron had somehow…changed. The wrinkles on Ron's brow began fading back into his taut skin. The crow's feet around his grey eyes seemingly disappeared, and the paunch of belly supporting his middle became slenderer in a blink of an eye. Catrina couldn't explain it. Somehow Ron seemed…younger.

Ron let out a long, reminiscent sigh, then continued.

"Man, that was the same year I was elected Class President and never told my Mother. Boy, was she ever madder than the Dickens at me! I came home from practice one day, and she was hootin' and hollerin' about me having something to tell her…"

It was a very cold autumn evening, encroaching on winter's subtle commencement. Ron's mother was waiting for him at their doorstep, arms crossed above her pregnant girth. She was expecting soon; however, the joy in her face was more for her first born.

"And where have you been, young man?" She reproached Ron, teasingly as always.

"Mother, you know I attend practice every Tuesday and Thursday".

Ron's mother stood in front of the door, not budging an inch as he approached her.

"Have something to tell me, do you?"

Ron thought long and hard but couldn't figure out this latest puzzle his mother threw at him. He didn't think he did anything wrong. His grades were spot on, and all of his teachers loved him.

"Why, no, Mother. I don't think I do." Ron tried to sidle past his mother, only to be pushed backwards by her left knee, albeit softly.

"Ronnie," she started, "You don't lie now to your mother. You tell her this instant how you were elected Class President."

Ron blew out a sigh of relief and produced one of his infamous guffaws.

"Oh, that. Yeah, I guess so." Then he snuck past his mother, notwithstanding a kiss on her cheek, and hurried inside his home. His mother just stood there, bewildered at his youth, as always.

Catrina followed the retelling with ease but remained focused on the ever-changing features that were displayed right before her. As Ron expounded on his exchange with his mother, he seemed to shrink in his seat. The blue Air Force cap slid from his head onto the black and white checkered floor beneath him, and golden locks of hair began replacing the white tufts sections at a time. Ron's wiry mouth became fuller, as did the squareness of his chin. Catrina was fascinated.

Ron never noticed. He just continued telling his tales.

"I remember working here, at this diner. This was right after high school, and right before I joined the Air Force." Ron spoke with such enthusiasm now; however, his voice started to alter a bit and become softer. "My friend and I worked the counter, making floats for the kids coming home from school. I…I remember when we thought it would be a hoot to try something different…"

Ron and Mike were early entrepreneurs of their time. Mike's father owned the General Store across the street; a store that has since closed, and due to zoning, had been brought down to make room for other developments. But this General Store was one of the few that sold beer. And back during Ron's days, you could buy beer at age 18.

Ron sent Mike over to the store one particular hot summer day to pick up a six-pack of some cheap beer. Of course, Ron had a *wonderful* idea.

"Mike," Ron said, "I'm tired of just root beer floats. Today, we are going to make some boozy floats! Go get us some beer, and let's see if we can freeze it enough to make something delicious!"

So, Mike went across to his father's store, picked up a six-pack, and brought it back to the diner. What happened next was told to the owner and the police in two separate reports. For starters, the two boys were schnockered before noon, while on the job. The alcohol never froze, and caused the actual ice cream (vanilla bean, to be precise) to quickly foam and escape the mugs upon being poured over. While the beer spilled, the flooring became slippery, which caused the drunken boys to slide and fall, breaking bottles, part of the countertop, Mike's wrist, and their pride. The boys no longer worked at the diner after that day; however, Ron's guffaws were so loud, so serene, and so incorrigible, that all who witnessed the scene could do nothing but join him in laughter. Neither parents were notified.

Catrina removed her hat and ran her black fingernails through her cropped black hair. She still could not believe what she was witnessing. Ron's ears lowered, his hair grew, his skin tightened, his muscles toned. Even his teeth whitened and sparkled as he smiled. Anger and astonishment raised in her purple (blue) eyes.

"Ronald, darling," she teased him, "It's about time we got going. How about you finish your pie?"

"Oh, the pie!" Ron burst out with another of his famous guffaws. "I almost forgot about how much I love the pie here. Why, every time I came home from the Air Force, my lady and I would come here, and I would just gobble up a slice of pie before we left! She told me I'd have my last meal here if I ever had my choice."

Ron entered the service shortly after the incident with the beer floats. He studied hard, and trained even harder, enough to become a dashing young pilot in the military. Flying combat missions over Korea, and some in Vietnam were fun for Ron; that was, until he met who would become his bride.

He met his old lady during a church function down in Texas. The two love birds were only together for a few days before Ron was deployed out yet again. Ron spent most of his days flying over enemy camps, and his evenings catching that bird on the wire, talking with the one he loved. Although he always thought she was out of his league, Ron still proposed to her, one night while forwardly deployed somewhere in the vast regions overseas. And of course, she said 'yes'. Ron suspected that his wife had somewhat of a wanderlust; he thought she only married him for the travel and adventure.

"But we always seemed to come back here." Ron finished, reminiscing about his long-lost time with his wife. "We'd eat our supper, and I'd order the same thing to cap it all off: a slice of apple crumb, and a root beer float. Boy, those were the good ol' days."

Catrina knew it was now or never, so she cut into the pie herself and attempted to feed Ron a hunk.

"That's good, Ron. Just like old times, right? I bet this pie tastes just like you remember".

Ron looked at the pie, then looked at the clock on the wall.

"Holy smokes, lady!" He said with a start. "I'm going to be late!"

Catrina looked at him, confounded. Gone was the 86-year-old geezer she had come for. Instead, a dashing late teenager stood in his place. A worrisome, dashing young teenager, twisting the blue Air Force cap in his hands without even glancing at it. He refused to eat the pie, nor even touch the now warm root beer float. Time had marched on from morning to mid-afternoon. But for Ron, it seemed to backwards peddle decades.

"Late for what, Ronald? We still have business to attend to." Catrina became impatient, as foretold by the daggers in her glance.

Ron looked at her as if for the first time. Had he seen this woman before? Perhaps in his dreams. His mother never mentioned anyone so strikingly beautiful moving into the neighborhood. Where had she come from?

"Ma'am?" Ron stammered. "Do I know you? Can I help you with something?"

Catrina could hold her tongue and sardonic appeal no longer. She snapped her lithe fingers, and from beyond the kitchen's doors came the delicate sound of guitar playing and heavy cowbell, Blue Oyster Cult's infamous 'Don't Fear the Reaper'.

"Ronald, I am Catrina. The Lady of Death. You made a promise way back when that you would have your last meal here at this very diner. I am here to see to it that you keep your word."

Ron's face shriveled. Then he let out the loudest, honking guffaw of his teenage life.

"Lady, I have no idea who you are, or what you are talking about. What I do know is that I am late for the football game. Today we are taking on the Cootesville Cougars, and the coach is counting on me to see us through to victory. I don't have time to yammer with you anymore. I have to go!"

Ron bustled from his stool and tried to run past Catrina. Catrina held a long, creamy white arm out in front of him, and kept Ron in her purple-blue gaze.

"Take my hand, Ronald", she said, plainly. "We must go at once. It is time for me to take your soul."

Ron looked her over and smiled.

"Lady, I don't think so. I still have a full life to live."

Catrina grabbed him by the lapel of his shirt.

"YOU ARE COMING WITH ME, BOY!" She

screamed.

Ron just smiled, holding in his appreciable laughter.

"Not in this life." He replied.

And with a snap of his own fingers, Ron disappeared.

Catrina looked down at the heap of old man clothes gathered at her feet; the button-down shirt remained in her fingertips at the collar. With a gentle moan, Catrina spun on her heels and walked out of the diner.

Time seemed to never stand still in that suburban town. What was once a blissful morning developed into to a crisp autumn evening. As the stars began to twinkle, Catrina unfurled her leathery wings and took flight into the night sky.

NIGHTMARES

Father checked the closet, vanity, and under the bed, but could not locate the monster devouring his daughter.

A MONSTER ATE MY HOMEWORK

Emily was just like any other young adult, yet teenage girl. Average height, medium build, mousy features. Even her straight, dusty blonde hair dared not compare to the rays of the sun; for that, as it seemed, would just stand her out from the crowd. No, Emily was just as plain as the pale skin she adorned, even plainer than her slate-grey eyes, or the smallest of noses settling on her face. But this never bothered Emily. She enjoyed being nondescript.

It was mid-October when the rumors began. Emily never minded about such trivial things. But her classmates started pondering the mysteries surrounding Emily's past. And the subtle, yet recurrent marks that appeared upon her delicate arm.

Emily lived in a rural town, just east of a flowing civilization filled with suburban mediocracy. She resided with her father, a Post 9/11 Veteran who returned from the war with medals, an Honorable Discharge, and a wheelchair. Emily was his primary caregiver; her mother had died of leukemia shortly after she was born, and she spent countless hours wondering if she even looked anything like her. She knew she resembled much of her father, which was certain. Straight down to her demeanor; a little reserved, sometimes on edge, always with her head on a swivel.

Her father lived disability paycheck-to-paycheck, able to afford their lot rent for the single-wide donated to them when he returned from the service. Food was never sparse; however, most of the money went towards his care. Trips to the VA, medications that the VA refused to pay for, his alcohol abuse. He never drank in front of his daughter, but she knew he did so to cope with his demons. She could smell the aftereffects lingering early in the morning.

Emily was your average high school student. A few B's and C's, some tardy days, and absences here and there (mainly due to taking care of her father). For the most part, Emily kept to herself. She did not host any friends that she could really claim as such. And as far as interests in boys? Sure, there were a few that she thought were cute, and perhaps she had a crush on one. But her focus had to remain on her father. He needed her now, more than ever. She was, as it were, 'Daddy's Little Girl.'

This school year proved rather difficult for Emily. For starters, she was just about to turn eighteen in a few weeks; oldest in her class, but not because she was left behind or that she failed out of any of her grades. Timing due to her father's deployments, foster care, homeschooling…it all took its toll on her. So senior year provided its challenges, while still fulfilling its own rewards. Emily knew she had many choices for college. Her father paid the ultimate price for that; she could go anywhere, study anything on the government's dime. Just if she made it through this year.

Most of the other girls in class were stuck-up snobs. They either paid Emily no mind or minded her too much as to make sure her life was a living hell.

Constant chatter during class about Emily being a slut. About the entire basketball team. Emily wasn't even a fan of basketball, let alone any sports. She'd come home from school, isolated and depressed, and then must face her father.

"Em, is that you?" Her father would start in, knowing it had to be his little girl. Who else would want to break into their meager little home?

"Yeah, Dad." She'd reply, knowing how the game would start.

"What's wrong with my girl?" Her father always had an innate sense about him. If only he knew where that damned landmine was before he stepped, he would still have his legs.

"Nothing." She'd reply, knowing he could see right through her lies.

"Now, Em, you know that's a lie." He retorted. "You know I despise a liar. Come sit with me and tell me about it."

"I…I don't want to talk about it, Dad." Emily stated, shakiness taking over her voice. She knew what was coming.

"Em," her father coaxed, not unkindly, "Please come here. And bring the paddle with you."

The next day at school, Emily sported the first bandage across her arm, covering a bloody welt that wasn't there the day before. The noise from her classmates increased, and the rumors spread like wildfire. Emily spent some time with counselors, which she explained that everything at home was 'fine'. Emily spent the next 3 days absent from school, complaining of her monthly, to get her through until the next week without ridicule. This way, she could continue to take care of her father.

Upon her return to classes the week after, Emily was faced with more homework, more studying, and yes, even more ridicule. Even the boys started their own repartee. Saddest of all, the boy she was crushing on was leading the pack. Emily cut class after 4th period and rushed home, hoping her father wouldn't notice her own early dismissal. Of course, he did.

"Em, is that you?" Let the games begin.

"Daddy, I don't want to talk, ok? Just leave me alone!" Emily rant to her room, crying all the way.

Her father gave chase as fast as his standard wheelchair and upper body strength would allow.

"Em!" he beckoned. "Open the door, hon! It's me, your father! Please?!"

Emily reluctantly opened the door, tears streaming from her eyes. Her father wheeled inside her room.

"Em, did someone hurt you? What happened?"

"Nothing, Daddy. I'm fine." Emily wiped fiercely

at her face, reddening her cheeks with her sleeves.

"Now Em." Her father reproached her. "You know I despise a liar. You also know what that means."

Her father began to take off his leather belt, slowly unlooping it from his dirty blue jeans until he had it firmly in his grasp.

The next day, Emily returned to class with more bloodied welts on her arm, poorly bandaged. She was downtrodden, embarrassed, and tired. Again, the counselors came to her out of concern. And again, she told everyone that she was 'fine'. She stayed the entire day at school this time, determined to face her own demons while learning a thing or two. What she did learn was that she had quite a bit of ground to make up in math and could do so for homework.

When Emily came home, she could tell right away two things: One, she would have to complete her homework in a room far away from the crushed cans and vomit; Two, her father was drunk, again.

"Em, 'ish dat youf?" Her father tried to make words, but she knew the drill easy enough.

"Yes, Dad. I'm home. Let's get you cleaned up, Ok? I have some homework to do." She sounded so confident, so in control.

"Daffy's Lil' Monturd?" He tried to say. Monster? She smiled at that. He hadn't called her a 'monster' since she was three.

"Yes, a little monturd". Emily started cleaning up the mess, wheeling her father away from the clutter and retch and into the small bathroom that they shared. She helped him undress, and sat him upon his shower-seat, turned on the water, and pulled the curtain so he could have some privacy while he bathed himself. She sat on the broken toilet seat just in case he needed help with anything. Luckily, he didn't. After drying off, her father dressed in his lounge clothes and returned to his wheelchair. By then, he was starting to snooze. Emily took advantage of the time and started on her homework.

Math was never an easy subject for Emily; however, it was something that her and her father could always tag-team and get through.   This homework was a breeze, and Emily felt so proud to be able to get through it in no time. It was a good thing too, since sleep was not an easy subject for her lately, either. Emily laid the finished homework (a one-pager) on the kitchen/dining room table for her father to gloat at in the morning, and took herself to bed, finally feeling a sense of accomplishment.

A lone gunshot woke her from her slumber. Emily raced to the kitchen/dining room area, and found her father, sitting in his chair with his head held high, a large exit wound coming from the top of his head through his open mouth. Her father's .45, a hand-me-down from his grandfather, was still smoking from the single bullet fired from its chamber. Blood splattered everywhere, covering all surfaces of the miniscule table they owned. Including the math homework Emily left for her father to review. Emily fell to her knees, not knowing what to do, not knowing what to say. Not knowing if she could even cry.

It took Emily a little while to process everything that happened, but she finally realized that her father left her a note on the back of her math paper. She rubbed her tearless eyes and read the words through the blood that was starting to stain:

"My Dearest Emily,

I am so sorry for failing you as a father. After all of these years, when you needed me the most, I was never there for you. I tried, honey. I really did try. Every time that you needed to get your aggressions out, I allowed you to take it out on my broken-down body. I gave you the tools; the paddle, whips from the switches found outside, my belt, your knife. Yes, I have known about your knife for some time now and know that you cut yourself. I wish you didn't waste your time trying to care for me, and just live your life the way you are supposed to. The way your mom would have wanted you to.

Maybe if I wasn't here, you'd no longer have a choice.

I love you, Emily. You will always be Daddy's Little Monster".

Love,
    Dad"

That last line finally brought Emily to tears. Through silent sobs and snot, Emily started tearing the note apart. Then, surprisingly, she ate the paper, digesting the evidence.

"I love you too, Daddy."

Emily walked into school the next morning, a wreck of a person she once was. A fresh bloody welt raised up on her arm, resembling eleven numbers in a sequence: 18002738255. She brushed past her counselors, who called the Department of Social Services immediately upon laying eyes on her. She was in math class when Child Protective Services came to the door, right about the same time the authorities found her father dead at the scene. Before Emily was taken into custody, her math teacher asker her where her homework was.

"My homework?" Emily asked. "Oh. A monster ate it."

ABOUT THE AUTHOR

Originally from the suburbs of eastern Long Island, NY, Salvatore J. Lo Monaco is a Disabled, Medically Retired Veteran of the United States Navy. His love for writing (mostly dark fiction, fantasy and poetry) stems from the second grade; however, he never felt compelled to intimately share his works until now.

When not writing, Sal spends most of his time building Lego sets, daydreaming, and destroying silence as an 80's Hair Metal/Glam Rock drummer.

Sal now resides in Hendersonville, NC with his wife Misty, his daughter Bella, five dogs, a cat, and a hedgehog.